THE BREAK THROUGH

CARLA MARRERO

Prologue

So here I am again in a state of
doubt and shaky ground.
I am thankful for where I am but
little things throw me off.
In my heart I have roots of unbelief.
When a trigger goes off I fall short.
It always happens at the height of
my spiritual walk. Regardless, I will
continue this graphic novel.
I'm not the the only one who feels this way.
Maybe someone who reads it won't
feel so lost and isolated.
We are meant to suffer together.
As we do, we build each other up knowing
through pain, we are loved and never alone.

Godbless,
Carla Marrero

"I just go down again and again. Peace isn't an option for me."

"Don't beat youself up. Stop listening to lies."

"I try but the worst of me always wins. I'll never –"

"STOP!!! You are wonderful and blessed with purpose!
Shift your gaze on what you are made for."

"That's hard to do. I hope I'm not a burden coming to you like this."

"You are never a burden.
I know this will be hard but I will suffer with you,
I promise."

WARFARE CHRONICLES

TO BE CONTINUED...

Bottom Feeder

While I am down here I can look up
but that is where it stops.

At the bottom I can not hear but
I feel safe.

You see my friends below have settled
for what they are so why shouldn't I?

There is a beauty in the familiar sting
of the cold ocean floor.

Yet sometimes, gleams of light trickle
down through, tickling my blue skin.

Could there be more for me on
the surface?

WARFARE CHRONICLES

your burdens are crushing you but they dont have to. Want to unload them?
TO BE CONTINUED...

Little Boy Running

He runs into fields of emptiness.

As he moves his mind is light but
his heart is heavy.

If he stops running he will have to
face the heaviness.

Something too painful to do alone.

There was a time when he didn't run.
His heart was a feather, laughing with
the breath of angels.

Now he tries to out run the darkness within
through emptiness leading him nowhere.

Until he stops and takes a much needed
breath,

He will keep running.

Until he can see that he can still laugh with
angels,

He will keep running.

Little boy stop running.

Heaven has you in the darkness!

WARFARE CHRONICLES
To be honest, the load is on me because I'm drawn to it.
At first it appears luscious. The first taste is gratifying but...

...not enough. I Keep biting until the load has taken root. I'm so rooted in the coldness that I can't remove this Crown—
You have to cut the source of the roots first.

WARFARE CHRONICLES

There is always MORE.
TO BE CONTINUED...

TOXIC TABLE

Her weary face says it.
She needs water to live.
However, a broken heart bleeds
poisoned blood.
Blood from brokeness saturates
the water table in the ground with
contamination.
So as her roots absorb much needed
water, it is polluted with her own
anger, bitterness, pain, regret and shame.
She survives on this cycle but does not live.

Life vibrantly burns around her,
but she never takes notice.
If she only new how strong
her roots really are.
If she only rooted them in forgiveness, mercy,
peace, joy and grace.
Then she would branch out and bud into
the beauty she was meant to be.

WARFARE CHRONICLES

You need honest water to wash away the lies from the load of fruit you've eaten.
TO BE CONTINUED...

DOORWAY HOME

Where did this door come from?

I don't know. Where does it go to?

There is a lot of light coming from it!

I know, it feels warm too!

Let's try to open it. I'm tired of the dark!

But what if it isn't safe?

What if it is? I'm tired of being lost
and scared.

You think we can find our way home
through this door?

Maybe. It might take us there. We can't get
there if we stay here!

Okay let's try to open it! I want to go
home where I won't feel sick anymore!

WARFARE CHRONICLES

EMBRACE IT!

The Break Through

It's amazing to feel what I'm experiencing!
I've never been alive before.
I've been a pile of bones deep underground
for as long as I could remember.
The hardness of stones were always
my comfort.
One day, as water trickled down,
the soil bewteen the stones began to change.
It was moist and nourishing.
Suddenly my bones assembled into a strong
foundation.
Then I dared to do something I've never done.
I wriggled my way to the surface
breaking through.
The light on me ignited a warmth in my bones.
Muscles of strenghth and organs of life formed.
Skin of protection sealed my body holding
me together.
Nothing feels better than breaking free of
weighty rocks.
Now I break through and embrace the life
I was built for.

Dedications

I dedicate this graphic novel to so many
loved ones who set me on the right path.
Some of you are still here, some of you
have passed on. Regardless, you made a mark
on my life and heart. You suffered with me,
listened to me and accepted me.
God has blessed me greatly through
your open arms and guidance.
I see how fearfully and wonderfully made I am
and I thank You.

I also dedicate this graphic novel to
those who never suffered well, sinking
to rock bottom. Who didn't have someone
to trust and fight for them. Who saw the
dirt before the gold in themselves. Who
wore masks to hide their pain and regrets.
It may be hard to see now but you are
made to look up to God and breathe new life.
You owe it to yourself to let go of the past
and walk in freedom!

Isaiah 43:18-19

www.ingramcontent.com/pod-product-compliance
Lightning Source LLC
Chambersburg PA
CBHW042136120726
47911CB00022B/100